WAYANS FAMILY PRESENTS
THE BOO CREW

A Miracle on D-Roc's Street

Written By
Shawn Wayans
Marlon Wayans
Keenen Ivory Wayans

Printed in the U.S.A.

Chapter 1
The ShortCut

The city was alive with fresh snow and holiday shoppers in the streets. Christmastime was finally here!

The holiday spirit filled the air as the Boo Crew made their way toward their favorite Christmas spot, Messy's department store.

"I don't remember Messy's being this far," said D-Roc. "Slim, you said this was a shortcut."

"It is," said Slim. "We cut through McBurgers, Earl's Jr., and Pizza World."

Slim was busy stuffing an egg roll into his hamburger, which was wrapped in pizza. Then he put the whole thing in his mouth!

As Slim was chewing he said, "Two . . . *chew* . . . *smawk* . . . more . . . *crunch* . . . restaurants and . . . *gulp* . . . we'll be there!"

Dee Dee gave Slim a gross-me-out look. "We need to hurry up. I can't wait to see Santa face-to-face so I can tell him what I want."

"You don't need to see him face-to-face," said D-Roc. "With your big mouth, he can hear you from the North Pole!"

"BWAAAAHHHAAAAHAHAHAAAA!" the Boo Crew laughed.

"D-Roc, we ought to spell your name C-O-R-N," Dee Dee shouted.

"Why's that?" asked D-Roc.

"Because your jokes are CORNY!" teased Dee Dee.

"Oh, SNAP!" yelled Slim with his mouth full. "All this talk about corn is making me hungry."

The Boo Crew started laughing harder and D-Roc looked really embarrassed.

"Oh, yeah?" said D-Roc. "Just for that, you

can't play with my new G-Bot that I'm
getting for Christmas."

"So, G-Bots are stupid," snapped Dee Dee.

"No. They're hot," cried D-Roc. "I think I can
freestyle about them. Hit it, Dirty!"

Dirty had been standing in one patch of snow so
long it had turned black! He raised his hands to his
mouth and started to beat-box.

Boom-boom-tap, boom-boom-tap, boom-boom-tap,
boom-chicka-chicka-chicka . . .

D-Roc went into his freestyle rap:

"I'm building a snowman with my new G-Bot toy.
His name is Mega G and he's full of Christmas joy.
'Cause it's Christmastime, I'm bustin' Christmas
rhymes. With a flow so strong I can stop on a . . .
on a . . . *quarter?*"

Suddenly D-Roc was pelted by one big snowball, as all the Christmas shoppers in the street yelled, "DIME!"

Chapter 2
The Line to Santa's Lane

Messy's department store was jam-packed with last-minute shoppers. Everyone's arms were full of presents.

The Boo Crew ran through the crowd to be the first in line to see Santa. But when they got there, the line was already long!

"I don't know what all the hype is about Santa Claus," said D-Roc. "Everyone knows he doesn't really exist."

There was a huge *POP* over the PA speakers, and the Christmas music suddenly stopped. The Boo Crew froze and all the shoppers in Messy's department store turned to look at D-Roc.

"Yo, D-Roc, why are you hatin' on Santa like that?" asked Slim. "Who do you think buys and delivers those cool Christmas toys for us?"

"Our parents, that's who!" said D-Roc.

"I don't know about you, but I've never seen my parents come down the chimney! Ha-ha, yeah!" Dirty yelled.

"Maybe not, but it looks like *you* sure did!" Gwenny laughed.

Dirty's huge dirt cloud floated above Gwenny until, *POOF*, she was covered in filth!

"EEEEWWW! Why don't you ever wash, Dirty?" Gwenny coughed. "Ugh, how can anybody have a white Christmas when you're around!"

"D-Roc, look, the line is moving! Let's go!" yelled Dee Dee as she ran toward Santa.

"Man, if I believed in Santa, the first thing I would ask for would be a new sister," said D-Roc. "I'd get one that was really quiet and did all my homework for me, did all my chores, and knew all the cheats for my video games."

Just then Dee Dee rushed back over and said, "Oooh, D-Roc! This little itty-bitty boy just cut in front of me! I told him, 'Don't do that,' and he said, 'What are you going to do about it?' And I said, 'I'll tell my brother,' and he said, 'I don't care, tell your brother, I'll knock him out!'"

D-Roc looked at a little nerdy boy dressed in an elf costume and yelled, "Who said that, him?! I'll teach him to mess with my sister!"

Dee Dee shook her head, pointed her finger, and snickered, "Nope. Him!"

D-Roc looked up to find the biggest kid in the whole store staring down at him. The kid was grinding his teeth, cracking his knuckles, and flexing his massive chest muscles.

"You're going to beat me up?" asked the giant kid.

"N-n-no, of course not, you've got it all wrong. I didn't say I would beat you up. I said we should let that nice kid cut," whimpered D-Roc.

"So then, you're calling me a liar!" the giant kid screamed and chased after D-Roc.

"I really wish I could ask for a new sister!" D-Roc yelled as he ran from the giant kid. "Why can't you ever pick on someone my own size?"

Dee Dee smiled and said, "Because it wouldn't be as fun to watch, big bro."

Meanwhile, Gwenny sat down on Santa's lap.

"Well, what do you want for Christmas, little girl?" asked Santa.

"I have a bone to pick with you, Mr. Kringle. You work those poor little elves way too many hours, and they need a break!"

Santa chuckled and said, "You are absolutely right. I'll give them a break, starting today."

"Forget that! They need to make my Christmas gifts first!" said Gwenny as she walked off in a huff.

Slim jumped on Santa's lap.

"And . . . what . . . would . . . you . . . *gasp* . . . like . . . young . . . man," Santa struggled to say as his legs were shaking, trying to hold Slim's weight.

"I want Charlie's chocolate factory," said Slim.

"The movie or the book?" gasped Santa.

"Neither. I want the whole factory. Hmmm, and a glass of milk, too." Slim smiled.

D-Roc finally got back in line with his sister.

"D-Roc, aren't you going to sit on Santa's lap?" asked Dee Dee.

"No. Santa is for little kids like Gavin," D-Roc explained. He pointed to a little boy who was sitting in Santa's lap.

Gavin's clothes were old and torn. He looked very happy to be talking to Santa Claus.

"Santa, I want a job for my daddy and a smile for my mommy. Ever since my dad lost his job, my mom has been crying a lot," Gavin said. "As for me, I just want a G-Bot."

Then Gavin reached into his pocket, pulled out
a small, gift-wrapped box, and gave it to Santa.

"And this is for you, but remember, don't open it
until Christmas." Gavin smiled and ran off. Santa
put the present in his pocket, while the rest of the
Boo Crew watched Gavin leave.

Chapter 3
Chill, B.

On their way home from Messy's, the Boo Crew started talking about Gavin.

"*¡Aye caliendo!* Did you see Gavin give that gift to Santa?" cried Lissette. "That was so sweet."

D-Roc frowned. "It was pretty dumb if you ask me."

"Well, nobody asked you, E-BOO-neezer Scrooge," said Dee Dee.

"Whatever. All I know is, it's better to receive than to give," said D-Roc.

Slim, eating another sandwich, turned to his stingy friend. "You got it all wrong, D-Roc. The saying is 'It's better to GIVE than RECEIVE.'"

"Oh, yeah?" called D-Roc.

He quickly snatched Slim's sandwich and started eating it.

"HEY?!" screamed Slim.

D-Roc smiled with his mouth full. "So how does it feel, Mr. GIVER?"

"Point taken," Slim cried. "Yo, next time use somebody else's food as an example. I'm hungry."

Across the street, the Crew heard a noise.

Some private-school kids were picking on little Gavin. There was one particularly mean boy with red hair like an angry carrot. His face was filled with freckles, and when he smiled, there was a thousand-watt glow from the braces on his big crooked teeth. This was Freddy Stickler!

Every evil private-school kid has a sidekick, a henchman in all of his bullying and cruel pranks. And Sean Donovan was the perfect fit, with his huge ears, big feet, and skinny, skinny frame.

"Where are you going, you little bum?" teased Freddy. "The homeless shelter is closed today."

Sean laughed and the two boys started pushing Gavin back and forth between them.

"Yeah, your family is so poor, you fight pigeons for their bread crumbs!" yelled Sean.

"I'm not poor, my dad's just out of work right now," cried Gavin.

"Yeah, he's out of work and out of food and out of money," laughed Freddy.

The Boo Crew came running over to the bullies.

"Why don't you leave him alone, Freddy? Ain't nobody talking about those train tracks on your teeth," slammed D-Roc.

Freddy immediately turned as red as his hair with embarrassment as all the Boo Crew started laughing.

"CHOO CHOO!" they all started chanting.

"Oh, so you wanna play the Dozens? Well, your head's so big, I can see what you're thinking," said Freddy as he threw down a Dozens card.

Sean also threw down a Dozens card. The Boo Crew was not impressed.

"Your teeth are so spaced out, your toothbrush needs a map to find the next tooth!" said D-Roc as he threw down his Dozens card.

"Yeah, freckle face, your teeth so dirty, even your braces got cavities on 'em. Ha-ha, yeah!" cried Dirty.

Sean started laughing, but Freddy gave him a little elbow.

"What? It was funny," said Sean.

"You gonna let him talk like that to you, Sean?" Freddy asked.

Sean was confused. "No, I'm not gonna . . . wait a minute, you're the only one with braces."

"Oh," said Freddy, "come on, let's go."

Chad stepped forward when the bullies were far away and started his slams.

"Yeah, yeah? Well, you guys better run! You guys . . . you guys . . . you guys are so dumb, when you take your math test you score, like, a sixty-five, and then you almost fail social studies and your parents be all mad at you and stuff and they'll take your video games and make you eat vegetables . . ."

The Boo Crew fell silent.

"Yo, yo, Chad, chill, B. You makin' us look bad. I think they got the message," said D.J.

"Thanks for helping, you guys," said Gavin. "Even you, Chad."

"C'mon, we'll walk you home," said D-Roc.

"Uh, uh . . . No!" Gavin said nervously. "No, that's okay. I just live right up the street. I can make it from here, but thanks anyway."

Then Gavin ran down the street in the opposite direction. The Boo Crew all turned and started making fun of Chad for his bad slams, but D-Roc had something else on his mind.

And it didn't have anything to do with Santa Claus or bullies.

Chapter 4
MomMa's Christmas Decorating Skills

When D-Roc finally got home, his momma was yapping on the phone as usual.

"Yeah, girl, mmm-hmmm, busy is not the word. There was a two-for-one sale at the bakery and I stocked up. Talk about saving a little bread!" Momma cackled with laughter. "Well, girl, I got to go. It was nice meeting you. . . . How many times do I have to tell you! Juan doesn't live here. Okay, and a *gracias* to you, too."

"And where have you two been?" asked Momma.

"We stopped at the mall to see Santa Claus," said Dee Dee.

"Oh, and did you tell him what gifts you want him to bring you this year?"

"I did!" exclaimed Dee Dee. "But some people don't believe in Santa Claus, do they, D-Roc?"

"What's this? Now, D-Roc, we've been through this a thousand times. How do you expect to get gifts if you don't tell Santa Claus what you want?" asked Momma.

"I already gave YOU my list," said D-Roc.

As soon as the words came out of D-Roc's mouth, Momma's eyes rolled over.

"Anyway," Momma said, "it's time for Momma to decorate the Christmas tree. D-Roc, you go get the decorations, and, Dee Dee, you go get the popcorn and string. Then Momma's going to do the rest."

"I'll be right there," said Momma from the other room.

"Okay, Momma, we got the ornaments, the popcorn, and the string!" said D-Roc.

"That's good," said Momma. "Now take everything out of the box and line it up around the tree and Momma's going to do the rest."

D-Roc and Dee Dee started unpacking the ornaments and laying them out by the tree.

"Okay, Momma, everything is out of the boxes and lined up neatly by the tree," said Dee Dee.

"Good," said Momma. "Now string up that popcorn and put the lights and candy canes on the tree. Oh, and put up the ornaments, too. Momma will be in there in one minute."

"Okay, Momma," they said at the same time.

When Momma finally entered the living room, the Christmas tree was completely decorated.

Momma stepped up to the tree and pulled a star from behind her. She placed it on the top of the tree and stepped back to admire her work.

"OOO-WEE!" Momma hollered. "That tree is beautiful! Momma really outdid herself this time! That tree has got something to say!"

"Yeah, it's saying you should've helped," D-Roc whispered.

"Oh, there's my phone," said Momma as the phone started to ring.

Dee Dee and D-Roc let out a huge sigh. Christmas had officially reached their house.

Chapter 5

Under the Bed

D-Roc was in his pajamas. He looked right. He looked left. The coast was clear so he tiptoed out of his room.

D-Roc found Momma putting the finishing touches on wrapping presents.

"Santa Claus . . . yeah, right," D-Roc whispered to himself.

Momma hid the wrapped gifts under her bed and headed out of the room.

Quickly and quietly, D-Roc jumped into a military crawl and scrambled under the bed. He found a gift with his name on it and began to open it very carefully.

"Yes, a G-Bot!" D-Roc said to himself.

"D-Roc!" Momma suddenly screamed. "What do you think you are doing?"

"Um, nothing, Momma," D-Roc said from under her bed. "I was just . . ."

"Peeking at your gift," Momma said. "Don't try to lie to me, boy. You got that same look you had when you told me that lie about your dog eating your homework."

"But he did!" claimed D-Roc.

"Well, since you done ruined your surprise already, go ahead and open it," said Momma.

"But, Momma . . ."

"Go on," said Momma.

D-Roc reluctantly tore open his present.

"Oh, wow. A G-Bot," he said, faking his surprise.

"That's the last one they had at Messy's. I had to put a four-year-old in a full nelson for that G-Bot," laughed Momma.

"Thank you, Momma. I love you," said D-Roc.

"I love you, too, baby. And now it's time for my baby to go to bed," said Momma.

D-Roc went back to bed with his new toy.

MONEY The Cartoon

Chapter 6
Christmas Surprise?

The Boo Crew sat in front of D-Roc's stoop.

D-Roc came out of the front door with a cardboard box.

"All right, everybody, all aboard the Boo Crew Express!" he yelled.

The Crew rushed onto the sled. Slim gave them a push and down the hill they went. At first it was fun with the wind rushing around them. But then they lost control of the sled!

The Boo Crew headed toward an old building and they all began to brace themselves for a crash landing.

POW!

"WAAAHHH WOOHHH!" everyone yelled.

"Is everybody OK?" asked D-Roc.

"Aaahhhh! Not me! Aahhh!" screamed Dirty.

Everyone ran over to Dirty, scared that he might be hurt.

"My sneakers . . . my sneakers are scuffed!" he yelled.

Dirty licked his hand and wiped his bright white sneakers, which made them even dirtier.

As they were getting up to run the sled again,
they heard a familiar voice from an open window
above them.

"What do you mean we're not going to have
Christmas this year? I've been a good boy all year
long."

It was Gavin!

"Well, son, I just don't think Santa's going to come, because your father didn't . . ." Gavin's mom started to say.

". . . Give Santa our new address when we moved and . . . and he doesn't know where to find us," finished Gavin's dad.

"Yes, that's it," said Gavin's mom as she started to cry.

"Don't cry, Mom. We'll just go back to the mall and give Santa our new address," said Gavin. "Then everything will be all right. You'll see."

The Boo Crew all looked at one another.

D-Roc broke the silence. "Did you hear that, guys? Gavin's not gonna have a Christmas!"

MONEY The Cartoon

Chapter 7
Carols and Capers

"I know what we can do! Let's just do what Gavin said and give Santa Claus his new address," said Chad.

The Crew was back at their clubhouse, trying to come up with a plan to help Gavin.

"How many times do I have to tell you? There is no such thing as Santa Claus," D-Roc huffed. "His parents only told him that so they don't hurt his feelings."

"That doesn't mean Gavin shouldn't have a Christmas," said Dee Dee.

"Ya know, you're right. And I have a few ideas," schemed D-Roc. "Come on, you guys."

The Boo Crew went to Mrs. Robinson's building across the street. They were holding a sign that read: BOO CREW DECORATING SERVICE.

"Good evening, Mrs. Robinson. For a small donation, we would like to offer our Christmas tree decorating services," said D-Roc.

"That sounds very nice," creaked Mrs. Robinson.

The Boo Crew ran in and started decorating in a flurry. Soon they were standing around a fully decorated tree.

Dirty flipped on the light switch, and the tree came alive with a beautiful glow. But then, one by one, the lightbulbs all began to burst and the tree caught on fire!

"OUT, OUT, ALL OF YOU, OUT!" screamed Mrs. Robinson as she put out the flames with a fire extinguisher.

The Crew ran outside.

"Well, at least we got the money." D-Roc shrugged.

Suddenly Mrs. Robinson's hand came through the mail slot and snatched the cash back.

"Well . . . guess not," said D-Roc.

Next the Boo Crew went to Mr. Watkins's place. An old man opened up the door.

"Hello?" Mr. Watkins said in a loud voice.

D-Roc introduced himself, "Good evening, sir. For a small donation, my friends and I would like to sing you a Christmas song to help get you into the holiday spirit."

"That would be lovely. Let me turn my hearing aid up," said Mr. Watkins.

The old man gave money to D-Roc.

D-Roc turned toward the Crew and held his hands up like a music teacher. The Boo Crew began to sing "Carol of the Bells."

Their voices were like angels! For about five seconds . . . then the tape player behind them started going haywire!

Mr. Watkins heard the Boo Crew's real voices. And they sounded terrible!

Mr. Watkins grabbed his money back from D-Roc. "Y'all sound like a bunch of deaf seals!" he screamed. "Even I can hear that!"

The Boo Crew walked up to Mrs. Horan's brown-stone. Mrs. Horan, who was a sweet older lady, answered the door.

"Hi, Mrs. Horan. My friends and I were wondering if we could shovel the snow off of your walkway for a small donation?" asked D-Roc.

"Thank you, young man, but somebody already did it this morning," Mrs. Horan said as she closed the door.

"Huh? Who could be trying to take over the snow shovel business?" wondered D-Roc.

Chapter 8
Eyeverson's Christmas Tree

"Soo Young, how much did we make?" asked D-Roc.

"Well, we made a dollar fifty," said Soo Young.

"A dollar fifty? We can't buy any gifts with that!" said Dee Dee.

"But we can still GIVE him a nice Christmas," said D-Roc. "Everybody go home and pick one gift to give to Gavin. Let's meet at Gavin's at seven o'clock."

D-Roc and Dee Dee went to Cheapie's Tree Lot.

"Excuse me, sir, we're looking for a really nice tree for my friend. Can you help us?"

"All right, all right. Well, well, what about this one?" asked Cheapie. "It's a noble fir straight out of the redwood forest for a hundred dollars, all right?"

"You got anything less expensive?" asked Dee Dee.

"OK, OK, all right, calm down. All right. Over here we got a silver tip from the Swiss Alps, for fifty bucks, all right? Beat that."

"So, what can I get for this?" D-Roc showed Cheapie his money.

"HA-HA-HA-HA . . . for a dollar fifty?" laughed Cheapie. "All right, all right. I got the perfect tree for you. I got a green pine that's a little burned. Now, you might want to take your batteries out of your smoke detectors for the first three hours, all right?"

"But it's bald on one side!" D-Roc pointed out.

"Well, I'm sorry, kid. A dollar fifty's just not gonna get you Old Tannenbaum, all right?"

"Oh, don't worry about that," said Dee Dee. "With my hairdressing skills I can work with anything. Remember how bald Minzina was before I got ahold of her."

The kids bumped into Principal Eyeverson, who was also "eyeing" some trees for the holidays.

"Hey there, Principal Eyeverson, would you like . . ."

"No! I already bought some of your stale candy, son," said Principal Eyeverson.

"But . . ." said D-Roc.

"Do these look like the eyes of someone who's easily fooled?" asked the principal.

D-Roc attempted to look him in the eye but it was virtually impossible! Principal Eyeverson's eyes kept swirling.

"No, Mr. Eyeverson, it's D-Roc and Dee Dee from school," said Dee Dee.

"Oh, hey, kids, when did you get here?" Principal Eyeverson smiled.

"Happy Kwanzaa, boy," said Principal Eyeverson. "Oooh, you might want to ask Old Saint Nick for some lotion, son. Your hands are really dry."

"Uhh . . . Principal Eyeverson, we're over here," said D-Roc.

"Oh, tricky little fella, aren't ya," he laughed. "Why don't you help me get this Christmas tree to the car?"

"I see why they gave you a handicapped parking spot," said Dee Dee.

"I see what you're getting at, little missy! I know exactly what disability you're referring to," said Principal Eyeverson as he moved in very close to Dee Dee's face.

"It's my back!" he said. "Yup. I hurt it playing football back in college. Otherwise, I'd lift this whole tree lot without breaking a sweat."

Principal Eyeverson got into his car and started fixing his mirrors.

"Now, who in the world readjusted my mirrors? Darn Christmas pranksters!"

Principal Eyeverson turned his left mirror all the way right and down, then his right mirror all the way left and up. The mirrors had been perfectly adjusted for a normal driver!

"I think only Principal Eyeverson can see through these mirrors," laughed D-Roc. "I don't know what he's lookin' at, but it sure ain't people and other cars."

"Ahh, oh, that's better! Easy on the eyes. Well, kids, happy Kwanzaa and be safe!" Principal Eyeverson screeched off and crashed into cars parked along the street.

D-Roc and Dee Dee could hear him singing "Do you see what I see?" as he drove away.

Chapter 9
Breaking In and Decking the Halls

The Boo Crew gathered near Gavin's open window.

"Yo, how we gonna get in there?" asked Slim. "Nobody's home."

"We're gonna climb through the open window," said D-Roc.

"The only question is, who's gonna climb through the window?" asked D-Roc.

Everybody in the Boo Crew looked away.

"All right, all right. I guess I'll do it since I'm the smallest," said Slim.

The Boo Crew all stared at Slim like he was crazy.

"D-Roc, give me a boost," said Slim.

D-Roc came over and tried to pick up Slim.

"Hey, Chad, Dirty, D.J., help me give him a boost," D-Roc grunted under all of Slim's weight.

The whole gang came over and helped hoist Slim up and into the window.

"Wait, wait, yo, I'm stuck!" yelled Slim.

"Does anybody have any grease?" asked Soo Young.

"Looks like it's time for Dirty to do some dirty work! Ha-ha!" laughed Dirty.

Dirty wiped his oily body and gathered a handful of grease. He then spread it around the window and Slim.

The Boo Crew gave Slim a final heave and *THUD!* Slim was inside.

"Okay, I'm good," said Slim.

Just then Gavin and his parents arrived back home. They were standing in the hallway by the front door when Gavin almost started to cry.

"I'm sorry the mall was closed, son," said Gavin's dad.

"Don't worry, baby, it's just one Christmas," said Gavin's mom. "I promise you next year Santa will make sure you have the best Christmas ever."

When Gavin's dad opened the front door, their apartment was completely clean and spotless! There was a Christmas tree decorated with bright lights and ornaments. And under the tree were presents!

"I knew it!" Gavin screamed joyfully. "He found our house. I knew Santa wouldn't let us down! Wow! Look at all the gifts. And they have my name on them! Can I open them?! Please?!"

"Go ahead, son," said Gavin's dad, full of surprise and confusion.

Gavin tore into the pile of gifts underneath the tree.

"Oh, boy, look, Mommy, it's a pair of sneakers and a dirty rag. Cool.

"Look, a skateboard with an ice pack and a sling. This is awesome.

"It's a bean pie, a koufie, and an afro pick. Right on!"

Gavin picked up the last gift and began to open it. Before he got all the wrapping off he started jumping up and down in excitement.

"WOW! A G-Bot! This is the best Christmas ever!" he screamed.

"It sure is, son," Gavin's dad said as he embraced his wife lovingly.

Suddenly, a lovely Christmas carol was heard from outside.

Gavin and his family ran to the window. The Boo Crew were singing a well-rehearsed Christmas song.

"*Silent night, holy night.*
All is calm, all is bright . . ."

Chapter 10
giving is better

Back at home D-Roc and Dee Dee were getting ready for bed.

"You know, Dee Dee, seeing the excitement on Gavin's face gave me a warm feeling inside. It's true, 'giving is better than receiving,'" confessed D-Roc.

"I'm really proud of you, big bro," said Dee Dee. "You giving up your G-Bot like that is the true meaning of Christmas. Well, bro, I gotta get some sleep because tomorrow's Christmas and I gotta look cute when I open up my presents. Good night."

At seven A.M., D-Roc was sound asleep, until . . .

"D-Roc, wake up! It's Christmas!" screamed Dee Dee.

In the living room, Dee Dee excitedly ripped the wrapping paper off her gifts.

"Wow! I got a Beauty Salon! Oh, snap! A Gossiping Diary! . . . Oh, and a cute li'l baby-doll tee. Oh no, I know Santa didn't. I got a pair of Boom-Box Blades! I can skate and listen to music at the same time!"

D-Roc peeled the wrapping paper off his few gifts very slowly.

"Oh, wow, look, I got . . . socks," D-Roc said half-heartedly. "Would you look at that."

"All right, kids, time for me to clean up this mess. Momma got to do everything around here.

"Hold on a second. D-Roc? What's that over there?" asked Momma.

D-Roc saw one last gift leaning against the wall near the tree.

"I don't know. Probably another pair of socks," D-Roc said.

"Boy, I'm gonna SOCK you upside your head!" Momma yelled. "Now, what is that?"

He walked over to it and read the label. "Hey, it has my name on it." D-Roc smiled.

He ripped off the wrapping paper and started screaming, "OH, WOW! A MEGA G-BOT!"

There was a card stuck to the gift. It read: MERRY CHRISTMAS, D-ROC — LOVE, SANTA.

D-Roc heard bells jingling outside and ran to the window.

There was Santa Claus flying off in his sleigh.

"Ho-ho-ho! Merry Christmas, D-Roc! Merry Christmas to all!"

The End